Turtle-napped!

"Oh, great," Bess said. "The boys knocked down the whole snack table."

Nancy and Bess watched as doughnuts rolled everywhere. Then they ran to join George. George looked as if she had just seen a ghost.

"What happened?" Nancy asked.

"When I heard the crash, I jumped up to see what it was," George said. "I took my eyes off Harry for about a minute."

Nancy's mouth felt dry. "George? Are you saying that Harry—"

George shook the pink plastic case. The little door was open.

"He's gone!" George wailed. "Harry the turtle is gone!"

The Nancy Drew Notebooks

Available from MINSTREL Books

THE

NANCY DREW
NOTEBOOKS®

#29

Lights! Camera! Clues!

CAROLYN KEENE
ILLUSTRATED BY ANTHONY ACCARDO

**MINSTREL®
BOOK**

Published by POCKET BOOKS
New York   London   Toronto   Sydney   Tokyo   Singapore

A MINSTREL PAPERBACK *Original*

 A Minstrel Book published by
POCKET BOOKS, a division of Simon & Schuster Inc.
1230 Avenue of the Americas, New York, NY 10020

ISBN: 0-671-02463-9

First Minstrel Books printing February 1999

10 9 8 7 6 5 4 3 2 1

Cover art by Joanie Schwarz

Printed in the U.S.A.

QBP/✖

1

Trouble . . . Take One!

I think I've seen every movie Lucy Webb was in," eight-year-old Nancy Drew said.

"Wow!" Nancy's best friend Bess Marvin said. "That's a lot of movies."

Nancy's other best friend, George Fayne, whistled. "That's a lot of popcorn."

It was Saturday. A movie was being filmed right in River Heights. It was called *Totally Tina,* and it starred the girls' favorite nine-year-old actress.

A few days earlier, a group of kids from Carl Sandburg Elementary School had been picked to be in the movie. Three of them were Nancy, Bess, and George.

Now Mrs. Marvin was driving the girls to where the movie was being made.

"I heard that Jason, David, and Mike were picked, too," Mrs. Marvin said.

"The boys?" Bess groaned.

"I didn't know this was a *monster* movie," George said.

"Let's not think about the boys," Nancy said. "We're finally going to meet Lucy."

"*And* she's visiting our school on Monday," George added.

"I'm going to wear my new pink sweater on Monday," Bess said, twirling a strand of her blond hair. She turned to George. "What are you going to wear?"

George shrugged. "Whatever's clean."

Nancy smiled. Bess and George were cousins, but they were totally different.

Mrs. Marvin stopped the minivan on Main Street. "Here we are," she announced.

The girls climbed out of the van. They looked around with wide eyes.

2

"Are you sure this is Main Street?" Nancy asked. "It looks like Hollywood!"

Trucks and trailers were parked everywhere. Wires and ropes lay on the sidewalk. Every few feet there were cameras and lights.

"Welcome to the *Totally Tina* movie set," a woman wearing glasses said. "My name is Vera. I'm the director's assistant."

Vera showed the girls where to sign in. Then Mrs. Marvin arranged to meet them at the corner of Main Street in three hours.

"Does anyone see Lucy?" Bess asked as Mrs. Marvin walked back to the van.

"No. But here comes Rebecca Ramirez," Nancy said.

"I'm ready for my close-up, everyone," eight-year-old Rebecca called. She peeked over a pair of dark sunglasses.

George looked up at the sky. "It's not even sunny, Rebecca," she said.

"I know," Rebecca said. "But if I'm

going to be in a movie, I might as well look like a movie star."

Nancy knew that Rebecca always wanted to be an actress.

"Don't you hope this movie makes us all famous?" Rebecca asked.

"Nancy already *is* famous," Bess said. "She's the most famous detective in our school."

Nancy blushed a little. But Bess was right. She loved solving mysteries. She even had a blue detective notebook where she wrote down all her suspects and clues.

George pointed to the bright purple sneakers on Rebecca's feet. "Pretty cool sneakers, Rebecca," she said.

"Thanks," Rebecca said. "I read in a magazine that Lucy's favorite sneakers are purple. So I wanted a pair, too."

"Why?" Bess asked.

"Because I want to be just like Lucy," Rebecca said. She wiggled one sneakered foot. "From my head to my toes."

"Let's look around," Nancy suggested. "Maybe we'll find Lucy."

4

"Good idea," George said. But as they were about to explore the movie set, a boy shouted out.

"Stop! Don't move a single inch."

Nancy whirled around. It was Orson Wong, from their school.

"Why not?" Nancy demanded.

Orson pointed to a wad of gum stuck to the sidewalk. "Because I have to have *that*," he insisted.

"The chewed-up gum?" George asked.

Bess scrunched her face. "Gross."

Orson kneeled to scrape up the gum. He dropped it into a plastic bag.

"Nothing that once belonged to Lucy Webb is gross," Orson said. He held the bag open. "Check it out."

Nancy peeked inside the bag. "A scrunchie . . . a penny . . . a tissue?"

"It's my collection of Lucy Webb souvenirs," Orson said. "Neat, huh?"

"How do you know all this stuff belonged to Lucy?" Rebecca asked.

Orson grabbed the bag away. "Because I found it around her trailer, that's why."

The girls looked at one another.

"Orson has a crush on Lucy!" George sang. "Orson has a crush on Lucy!"

Orson's face turned bright red. "Will you pipe down?" he said. Then he turned around and ran down Main Street.

Rebecca gave a sigh. "There are big pests and little pests. Orson is somewhere in between," she said.

"And speaking of big pests," George said. "Look who's over there."

Nancy turned and saw Brenda Carlton standing in front of a trailer. She was tapping her foot impatiently.

"Don't tell me Miss Snooty Pants is in the movie, too," Rebecca said.

Nancy saw a pad and pencil in Brenda's hands. "She's probably writing some article for the *Carlton News*," she said.

"You mean the *Carlton Pe-ews*," Bess said with a giggle.

The *Carlton News* was Brenda's own newspaper. She wrote it at home on her father's computer.

Just then the door to the trailer swung open. A girl with curly brown hair stepped out.

"It's Lucy!" Nancy said excitedly.

Nancy, Bess, George, and Rebecca ran toward the trailer. Brenda jumped in front of them. She held up her hand.

"Back off!" Brenda shouted, waving her pad. "I saw her first."

The girls stared at Brenda as she stepped in front of Lucy.

"A few questions for the *Carlton News,*" Brenda said. "Is it true you pour orange juice on your cereal?"

"I'm sorry. I don't have time for an interview today," Lucy said politely.

"What!" Brenda gasped.

"How about tomorrow?" Lucy suggested.

Brenda stomped her foot. "Tomorrow is Sunday. I have a birthday party to go to."

"Give me a break," George muttered.

"I'm really sorry," Lucy told Brenda.

"So am I," Brenda said meanly. "And I hope *Totally Tina* is a *total flop!*"

Brenda flipped her long brown hair and stomped off.

"What's her problem?" Lucy asked.

Nancy shook her head. "She's just being Totally Brenda," she said.

Nancy, Bess, George, and Rebecca introduced themselves. Then Lucy had to leave to try on a costume.

"See you later," Lucy said. She looked over her shoulder and grinned. "Oh, and I don't pour orange juice on my cereal."

"She's really nice," Nancy said after Lucy left.

"Do you think she noticed my sneakers?" Rebecca asked.

"How could she not?" George asked. "You kept wiggling your foot."

"It was *asleep!*" Rebecca insisted.

Just then they heard Vera calling their names. "You're in the pizza parlor scene, girls," she said. "Follow me."

"Ye-es!" Nancy said excitedly.

Nancy hardly recognized the inside of Phil's Pizza Parlor. It was filled with cameras and lights. People wearing

Totally Tina caps scurried around everywhere.

"Hi, girls," a man with a beard said. "I'm the director, Steven Bluestone."

Rebecca held out her hand. "Rebecca Ramirez. Actress and future star."

Mr. Bluestone showed the girls to a table. On it was a hot, steaming pizza.

"Oh, great," George whispered as they sat down. "The boys are in this scene, too."

Nancy saw Jason Hutchings, David Berger, and Mike Minelli at a nearby table. They were laughing and sticking pieces of pepperoni over their eyes.

"Okay. Here's the scene," Mr. Bluestone called out. "Lucy just lost the big spelling bee. She runs into the pizza parlor and yells, 'Quick! I need an emergency pepperoni pie with extra cheese!' Any questions?"

Mike raised his hand. "Can we eat the pizza?" he asked.

"Yes," Mr. Bluestone said.

Rebecca raised her hand. "How about if I tell Lucy to order the mushroom instead of the pepperoni?" she asked. "And she's so grateful that we become best friends forever and ever and ever—"

"You don't have any lines," Mr. Bluestone interrupted.

Rebecca pouted and sank in her chair.

"Ha, ha," Jason snickered.

Mr. Bluestone gave a signal. The lights flashed on brighter than ever.

"And ACTION!" Mr. Bluestone shouted.

The door flung open. Lucy ran in.

"I just lost the spelling bee," she groaned. "I need a—"

"Eeeeeek!" Bess screamed. She jumped up from her seat. "Something is crawling on our pizza!"

2
Going . . .
Going . . . Gone!

"CUT!" Mr. Bluestone shouted.

The girls stood up and backed away from the table.

"There *is* something crawling on our pizza, Mr. Bluestone," Nancy said.

Jason leaned over the table. "It looks like a turtle," he said.

"It's Harry!" Lucy shouted.

The girls stared at Lucy as she picked up the turtle. It was almost three inches long.

"What is Harry doing on the set again?" Mr. Bluestone demanded.

Vera turned to a young man with freckles. "Arnold? Wasn't it your job to turtle-sit?" she asked.

12

Arnold held up a pink plastic carrying case. "He must have escaped again, Vera."

Nancy watched Lucy cradle Harry in her hands. "Is Harry your pet?" she asked.

Lucy nodded. "He goes everywhere with me. Even to movie sets," she said.

Rebecca leaned over and whispered to Nancy. "Purple sneakers . . . now all I need is a turtle to be just like Lucy."

Phil, the owner of the pizza parlor, shook his head. "I don't allow animals in here. Even if he is a star," he said.

"Harry's not a star," Lucy said. She pointed to Harry's back. "But he does have a star-shaped mark on his shell."

Nancy smiled. "And two little white dots on his head," she added.

"And icky cheese and tomato sauce all over his feet." Jason laughed.

"Kids," Mr. Bluestone called. "We have a movie to shoot, remember?"

Lucy gently placed Harry in his pink carrying case. "This time I'm closing both latches," she said firmly.

Nancy watched Lucy lock the case and hand it back to Arnold.

"Places, everyone!" Mr. Bluestone said.

"Here," Phil said when they sat down. He placed a fresh pizza on Nancy's table. "Extra cheese and no turtle feet."

The girls giggled.

"Take two!" Mr. Bluestone called.

"That's movie talk for, 'Let's do it again,'" Rebecca whispered.

The lights flashed on again. Mr. Bluestone pointed to the door. "And . . . action!"

During the second take, Lucy forgot her line. In the third take, Mike dropped a slice of pizza. The fourth take was great.

"That's a print," Mr. Bluestone said. "Thanks, everyone."

"There will be a fifteen-minute break," Vera announced. She turned to the girls and smiled. "You're done for today."

The boys grabbed their slices and ran out of the pizza parlor.

As the girls walked out, Nancy felt Lucy tap her shoulder.

"Nancy?" Lucy asked. "Can you watch Harry while I go to the makeup trailer?"

Nancy was too surprised to speak. Lucy Webb was asking her for a favor!

"I thought Harry goes everywhere with you," Rebecca said.

"He does," Lucy said. "But all that face powder makes him sneeze."

"Turtles sneeze?" George asked.

"I'll be glad to look after Harry," Nancy said quickly. She saw Rebecca flash her an angry look.

"Thanks," Lucy said. She handed Nancy the pink plastic case. "Take good care of him. I'll be back in a few minutes."

"Wow," Bess said after Lucy left. "Nancy is doing a favor for a movie star!"

"Nancy, Nancy, Nancy!" Rebecca said angrily. She put her hands on her hips. "I'm the best actress in school. Lucy should have asked *me* to look after Harry!"

"What does playing Tinker Bell in your class play have to do with watching a turtle?" George asked Rebecca.

"You just don't understand!" Rebecca said dramatically. She looked at her watch. "I have to go. It's time to meet my father."

The girls watched Rebecca walk away.

"Don't worry, Nancy," Bess said. "You didn't do anything wrong."

"I know," Nancy said. "And I'm going to take good care of Harry as I promised."

George pointed to a snack table. "And I'm going to get some doughnuts. Anybody want some?" she asked.

Nancy shook her head. "The powdered sugar might make Harry sneeze, too."

"I know," Bess said. "We'll bring you a doughnut without powdered sugar."

"Okay!" Nancy said. She watched Bess and George run toward the table.

Nancy was about to peek into Harry's

case when she heard two people arguing. She looked up and saw Mr. Bluestone and Vera.

"Vera, that turtle has got to go," Mr. Bluestone was saying. "Every time he escapes from his case we lose more time."

Nancy's mouth dropped open. Was the director talking about Harry?

"But Lucy loves Harry," Vera said. "And she did promise to lock both latches from now on."

"I don't care if she puts him in cement shoes," Mr. Bluestone said. "Find a way to get rid of that turtle for good!"

"Yes, Mr. Bluestone," Vera said.

Nancy hid Harry's case behind her back as Mr. Bluestone and Vera walked by.

Just then Bess and George hurried over with a chocolate doughnut for Nancy.

"The boys were hiding under the snack table," George said. "Mike tried to tie my shoelaces together."

Nancy was about to tell her friends what she had heard when Bess grabbed her arm.

"What is it, Bess?" Nancy asked.

"I think I just saw another famous movie star," Bess said excitedly.

"No way!" Nancy said.

"I have an idea," Bess said. "Let's see how many famous people we can find. Then we'll ask them for their autographs."

"That sounds like fun," Nancy said. "But I promised Lucy I'd watch Harry."

Bess looked disappointed.

"You two go," George said. "I'll stay here with Harry."

Nancy looked down at the case in her hand. "But I promised Lucy I'd watch him."

"Don't worry," George said. She nodded toward a nearby bench. "I'll sit right there with Harry's case."

"Come on, Nancy," Bess said. "How often do we get to meet real movie stars?"

Nancy thought about George's offer. Then she smiled. If she couldn't trust her best friend, then who could she trust?

"Thanks, George," Nancy said. She handed the pink case to George.

Nancy and Bess recognized lots of famous actors on the movie set. Soon they had four autographs each.

"We're on a roll!" Bess said, waving her autographs in the air.

Suddenly they heard a loud crash.

"What was that?" Nancy asked as they glanced around.

"Oh, great," Bess said. "The boys knocked down the whole snack table."

Nancy and Bess watched as doughnuts rolled everywhere. Then they ran to join George.

"How is Harry, George?" Nancy asked.

"H-Harry?" George asked.

Nancy stared at George. She looked as if she had just seen a ghost.

"What happened?" Nancy asked.

"Did the doughnut make you sick?" Bess asked.

George shook her head. Her dark eyes flashed.

"When I heard the crash, I jumped up to see what it was," she said. "I took my eyes off Harry for about a minute."

Nancy's mouth felt dry. "George? Are you saying that Harry—"

George shook the pink plastic case. The little door was open.

"He's gone!" George wailed. "Harry the turtle is gone!"

3

It's in the Bag

Harry *can't* be gone!" Nancy said.

"We'll find him," Bess said. "Turtles are slowpokes. How far can he go?"

The girls looked around the bench. They even crawled underneath.

"He's nowhere in sight," George said.

Nancy's stomach flipped over. "What will Lucy say when she finds out?" she said.

Bess pointed over Nancy's shoulder. Nancy stared at Bess. Then she spun around. Lucy stood right behind her.

"Find out what?" Lucy asked.

"Um," George said. "Harry might have taken . . . a little walk."

"You mean he's gone?" Lucy gasped.

Nancy bit her lip and nodded.

"But I trusted you," Lucy told Nancy.

"It's all my fault," George said. "I was watching Harry when he disappeared."

"We looked all over," Nancy said.

Lucy's eyes were as wide as saucers. "Harry's never escaped outside before. He could be anywhere by now," she said.

Bess patted Lucy's shoulder. "You'll find Harry. At least by the time you visit our school on Monday."

Lucy looked at the girls. "Do you all go to Carl Sandburg Elementary School?"

The girls smiled and nodded.

"You *are* still coming," George said. "Aren't you?"

"After what you did?" Lucy cried. "No way!"

"Lucy, wait!" George called as Lucy ran to her trailer.

"Oh, no," Nancy said. "The kids at school will never speak to me again."

"But *I* lost Harry," George said.

"It doesn't matter, George," Nancy said. "Lucy asked *me* and I let her down."

George leaned against the bench. "Oh, well," she said. "Who wants a snooty movie star to visit our school anyway?"

Bess shrugged. "Everybody."

Nancy stared at the bench. She couldn't believe that Harry escaped. Lucy had locked both latches on the case.

"Something seems fishy," Nancy said slowly. She walked to the bench and ran her finger along the seat.

"What are you doing?" George asked.

"Harry's feet were covered with tomato sauce from the pizza," Nancy reminded her.

"So?" George asked.

"So Harry would have left some sort of messy trail, right?" Nancy asked.

"That's for sure," Bess said.

"Maybe Harry didn't escape," Nancy said. "Maybe Harry was *stolen*."

"You mean turtle-napped?" Bess asked.

"Come to think of it," George said, "when I put the case on the bench, the door faced forward."

"Go on," Nancy urged.

"But after Harry was missing, the door was facing backward," George said.

Nancy snapped her fingers. "The turtle thief might have turned the case around to open it," she said.

"This is a real mystery," Bess said.

"Are you going to try to solve it, Nancy?" George asked.

Nancy nodded. "Someone has to find Harry. It's the only way Lucy will come to our school on Monday," she said.

"Too bad you didn't bring your detective notebook today," Bess said.

Nancy pulled the blue book from her jacket pocket. "Who said I didn't?"

"Way to go, Nancy!" George said.

Nancy opened her notebook to a fresh page. On the top she wrote,

"Where's Harry?" Right under that she wrote, "Suspects."

"Who would want a turtle that bad?" George asked.

"Kittens are much cuter," Bess said.

Bess and George looked over Nancy's shoulder as she wrote, "Vera."

"The director's assistant?" Bess whispered.

"She's so nice," George said.

"I heard Mr. Bluestone tell Vera to get rid of Harry," Nancy said. "It sounded like an order."

"No!" George gasped.

Nancy twirled her pencil as she thought. "Who else?" she asked.

"What about Brenda?" Bess asked.

Nancy shook her head. "Brenda left early. She probably didn't even see Harry."

Nancy thought for a while. Then she added Rebecca's name to the list.

"Why is she a suspect?" George asked.

"Rebecca was mad that Lucy didn't

ask her to look after Harry," Nancy explained.

"And Rebecca said she needed a turtle to be just like Lucy," George added.

Bess gave a big sigh. "Why doesn't she just curl her hair?"

Nancy checked her watch. It was time to meet Mrs. Marvin. The girls walked through the movie set to the corner of Main Street.

Suddenly Bess grabbed Nancy's arm. "Nancy! Look who's coming out of the Bow Wow Shop," she whispered.

Nancy turned toward the pet store. She saw Rebecca standing at the door with a paper shopping bag.

"That's weird," George whispered. "Rebecca doesn't have any pets."

"Unless she has a new turtle," Nancy said. "Named Harry."

The girls walked over to Rebecca.

"Hi, Rebecca," Nancy said. She pointed to the bag. "Did you buy anything new?"

"I—" Rebecca started to say.

Just then Mr. Ramirez popped his head out the door.

"Rebecca?" he said. "Can you carry one last thing for me?"

"Sure, Daddy," Rebecca said. She placed the shopping bag on the sidewalk and ran back inside the store.

The girls stared down at the bag.

"Should we peek?" George asked slowly.

"It's not nice to snoop," Bess said.

"I said, peek, not snoop," George said. "There's a big difference."

"Let's wait until Rebecca comes back out," Nancy said. "Maybe—"

But it was too late. George had already grabbed one handle of the bag.

"I want to see, too," Bess said. She grabbed the other handle.

There was a loud ripping sound as the bag tore in half. Everything inside spilled onto the sidewalk.

The girls stared at the ground.

"Nancy?" George whispered. "Do you see what I see?"

Nancy nodded. "A turtle tank, a bag of Turtle Chops, turtle toys," she said.

Bess picked up a bottle. "I didn't know turtles took vitamins," she said.

"Do you know what this means, Nancy?" George asked excitedly.

Nancy nodded. "Rebecca has a new pet. And it's a turtle!"

4

Turtle-napped

Rebecca *must* have stolen Harry," George said.

"Why else would she have all this turtle stuff?" Bess asked.

"What are you doing?" asked an angry voice.

The girls spun around. Rebecca stood behind them with her hands on her hips.

"You were snooping through my bag, weren't you?" Rebecca demanded.

"We were *peeking*," Bess said. "There's a big difference. Right, George?"

"I guess," George muttered.

Nancy looked at Rebecca's hand. She

held a pink plastic carrying case. It was exactly like the one Lucy had.

"Harry is missing," Nancy said.

"Lucy's turtle?" Rebecca gasped.

"Did you see him?" Nancy asked.

"Nope," Rebecca said.

Nancy couldn't hold back any longer. She pointed to the case. "Then who is in there?" she asked.

Rebecca smiled. She opened the door of the case and reached in.

"Ta-daa," Rebecca sang. She pulled out a turtle and held it up. "Meet Sylvia."

"Sylvia?" Nancy asked.

"The purple sneakers weren't enough," Rebecca said. "If I wanted to be just like Lucy I *had* to have a turtle, too."

"We know that," Bess said. "But how do we know your new turtle isn't Harry."

Rebecca placed the turtle into Bess's hand. "See for yourself," she said.

"Eeeewwww!" Bess cried. She quickly handed the turtle over to Nancy.

"Do you see a star-shaped mark on

her shell?" Rebecca asked Nancy. "Or two white dots on her head?"

Nancy shook her head. The turtle wasn't Harry at all. It was Sylvia.

"You thought I stole Harry, didn't you?" Rebecca demanded. "You probably even wrote my name in your notebook."

"Sorry, Rebecca," Nancy said. "But you did seem pretty mad before."

"I *was* mad," Rebecca admitted. "Until I realized something very important."

"What?" Bess asked.

Rebecca lifted Sylvia dramatically. "Someday I'm going to be a big star, too," she said. "And everyone will want to turtle-sit for *me!*"

"Oh, brother," George mumbled.

The girls helped Rebecca put everything into a new shopping bag. By the time they were done, Mrs. Marvin drove up.

Inside the van, Nancy crossed Rebecca's name out of her notebook. The only suspect left was Vera.

"We have to go back to the movie set to look for clues," Nancy said.

"But we were just there," Bess said.

Nancy shrugged and smiled. "Think of it as Take Two!"

Later that afternoon Nancy, Bess, and George got permission to ride their bikes to Main Street. On the way, they stopped to buy Panda Bars from an ice cream truck.

The girls leaned their bikes against a tree. They were about to unwrap their ice cream when two little boys walked over.

"Aren't those Orson Wong's six-year-old twin brothers?" George whispered.

Nancy nodded. "Yes—Lonny and Lenny," she whispered back.

"Why did the truck have to park in front of Orson's house?" Bess asked.

Lonny and Lenny stopped in front of the girls. They stood and stared at them.

"What do you want?" George asked.

Lonny pointed to the girls' Panda Bars. "Those!" he said.

"Get your own," Bess said.

Lonny and Lenny looked at each other and giggled. Then they began to sing: "We know something you don't know! We know something you don't know!"

"What?" Nancy asked.

"Orson's room is filled with neat Lucy Webb stuff," Lenny said. "Want to see it?"

"Orson isn't home," Lonny added. "So you'd have his whole room to yourself."

"No, thank you," George said. "We know all about Orson's gross souvenirs."

Nancy grabbed Bess's and George's arms. She gently pulled them aside.

"What is it, Nancy?" Bess asked.

"Orson might have added Harry to his collection," Nancy said.

Bess nodded. "Orson Wong—the perfect suspect," she said.

Nancy and her friends walked back to the Wong twins.

"Okay, lead the way," George said.

"Not so fast," Lenny said. He and his brother held out their hands.

Nancy, Bess, and George handed over their Panda Bars. The boys ripped open the wrappers at once.

"Our house is right over there," Lenny said. He pointed to a bright yellow house.

"Orson's room is the first one up the stairs," Lonny said through a mouth full of ice cream.

The girls walked quickly toward the Wong house.

"Oh," Lenny called after them. "And watch out for Orson's new pet!"

5

Monster in the House

Did he say new pet?" Nancy asked.

The girls stopped walking.

"Harry!" they cried at once. They ran to the house and rang the doorbell. Orson's mother opened the door.

"Hello, girls," Mrs. Wong said.

"Hi, Mrs. Wong," Nancy said quickly. "We heard Orson has a new pet. May we see him, please?"

"I'm sure Orson wouldn't mind," Mrs. Wong said. "He's so proud of that creature."

"Thanks, Mrs. Wong!" George said.

The girls hurried up the stairs. Nancy found a door with a sign on it: Orson's room. Keep out! This means you!

"He can't keep us out today," Nancy said. She opened the door. "He's not home."

The girls walked inside. George stepped on a plastic action figure. A pile of dirty socks lay near the bed.

"What a dump," Bess mumbled.

Nancy looked around. A poster of Lucy Webb was taped over Orson's desk. Pictures of famous magicians were taped to the walls. Nancy knew that Orson wanted to be a magician someday.

"Let's look for clues," Nancy said.

They walked around the room. Nancy found a table filled with jars and boxes. Each one had a label that read, Lucy.

The girls looked inside all of the boxes and jars. They found plenty of junk but no Harry.

"I'll check out his desk," Nancy said.

It wasn't easy. Orson's messy desk was covered with papers, pens, and notebooks. But then Nancy saw something else. It was a green plastic tank.

Nancy tried to look through the clear lid but it was covered with a sign. It read, World's Best Pet.

"Bess, George," Nancy called.

"What is it?" Bess asked as she and George rushed over.

Nancy tapped the lid. "Orson's pet is probably in here," she said.

"But we can't see through it," George said. "How do we know it's Harry?"

"There's only one way to find out," Nancy said. She pulled up the lid. Then she looked inside and gasped.

A green, scaly creature with bulging eyes stared up at her.

"Is it Harry?" Bess asked quickly.

"N-no," Nancy stammered. "It's—it's some kind of *dragon!*"

Nancy jumped back as the creature popped his head out of the tank. He gazed around the room and flicked out his tongue.

"He looks like he's going to breathe fire!" Bess screamed.

"Let's get out of here!" George said.

The girls raced for the door. But just as they were about to run out, they crashed right into Orson.

"Ah-ha!" Orson shouted. "Trying to find out my magic secrets, huh?"

"No way," Bess said.

"And your bratty little brothers said you weren't home," George said.

Lonny and Lenny peeked out from behind the door. They had mischievous grins on their chocolate-covered faces.

"I see you've met Taco," Orson said. He walked over to the tank.

"Taco?" Nancy asked.

"My pet iguana," Orson said. He lifted the reptile from the tank and placed him on his shoulder. The iguana's long tail flicked against Orson's chest.

"When I become a magician I'm going to pull Taco from a hat," Orson said.

"Most magicians use bunny rabbits," Bess said.

"Well, I'm not most magicians," Orson said. "I'm Orson the Awesome!"

The girls rolled their eyes.

"So what were you doing in my room anyway?" Orson asked.

"We were looking for a missing turtle," Nancy said. "Lucy's turtle."

Orson's eyes lit up when he heard Lucy's name. "I knew Lucy had a turtle," he said. "But I didn't know it was missing."

"So you didn't steal him?" Bess asked.

Orson shook his head. "But I'd love to find him. Then I'd be a hero."

Nancy decided to herself that Orson was no longer a suspect. He liked Lucy too much to steal her pet.

"Let's go," she told her friends.

"Wait!" Orson called. He held Taco a few inches from their faces.

"Want to hold him?" he asked with a grin.

The girls froze as Taco flicked his tongue and rolled his eyes. Then they charged out of the house without saying a word. When they finally reached their bikes, Nancy scratched Orson's name from her list.

"Orson is clean." Nancy sighed.

"But his room's a mess!" George said.

"I'm never going in a boy's room again," Bess said, still shaking. "You never know what you'll find."

Nancy, Bess, and George rode their bikes to Main Street. The movie equipment and trailers were still there.

As they parked their bikes, Nancy saw Mr. Bluestone and Vera.

"I don't want them to see us here," Nancy said. "Let's hide."

"Where?" Bess asked.

Nancy quickly looked around. There was plenty of space underneath a trailer.

"Under there," Nancy said.

"It's dirty!" Bess complained.

The girls slipped under the trailer and peeked out. They could only see Mr. Bluestone's and Vera's legs.

"Mmmmph," Mr. Bluestone was saying. "Dese arck gooth."

"Mmm-mmm," Vera said.

"It sounds like they're munching on something," Nancy whispered.

"They shouldn't talk with their mouths full," Bess whispered back.

Nancy strained her ears to listen.

"Vera, I've eaten turtles before but this one was the tastiest," Mr. Bluestone said.

Bess gave a little shriek. George clapped her hand over Bess's mouth.

Vera went on. "And the crunchiest. There's more where that came from in the makeup trailer."

"Excellent!" Mr. Bluestone said.

"Did you hear what they said?" Nancy asked after Mr. Bluestone and Vera walked away.

"They just ate a *turtle*," George said.

"Oh, no," Bess said. "Not Harry!"

6
Chewy, Gooey . . . Phooey!

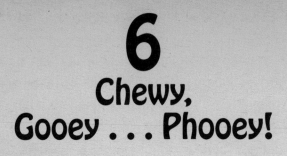

Who would eat a turtle?" Nancy asked as they crawled out from under the trailer.

George dusted herself off. "I once saw a TV show about food around the world. In one country they eat turtle soup."

"That is *so* gross," Bess said.

George shrugged. "Not everyone eats pizza and Panda Bars," she said.

"I know a way to find out if Mr. Bluestone and Vera snacked on Harry," Nancy said.

"How?" George asked.

"Vera told Mr. Bluestone there was more in the makeup trailer," Nancy said.

"Like what?" Bess cried. "Harry's shell?"

George shook her head. "That was probably the crunchy part," she said.

"Quit it, George," Bess complained.

Nancy looked up Main Street. In the middle of the block was a long trailer. A big sign on the door read, Makeup.

"There's the makeup trailer," Nancy said, pointing. "Let's try to look inside."

"Goody!" Bess said. "Maybe we can try on some makeup."

"Maybe *not*," George said.

The girls climbed the stairs to the trailer door. Nancy pulled at the handle. The door opened and she peeked inside.

"It's empty," Nancy said. She stepped inside. Bess and George followed.

A big mirror hung on the wall. It was framed with bright lights. There were three swivel chairs and a table filled with cases of eyeshadows and tubes of lipstick.

"Lipstick!" Bess said as she ran toward the mirror.

"Forget that," George said. She pointed to an open box of caramels on the table. "Check out the candy."

Nancy saw a pretty blue hat hanging on a hook near the mirror.

I wonder if Lucy ever wore this, Nancy thought. She reached for the hat and tried it on.

"How do I look?" Nancy asked.

"Totally glamorous," Bess said. "There's just one thing missing."

Nancy giggled as Bess brushed pink powder on her face. "Bess, that tickles!"

Just then the trailer door opened. A man and a woman stepped inside. They were wearing black smocks.

"Hi!" the woman said. Her red hair was almost pink. "I'm Lily and this is Max."

Max pointed at the girls. "You must be the kids for the next scene," he said.

Nancy didn't know what to say. She quickly grabbed the hat off her head.

"We . . . uh," Nancy said.

"Do we get to wear makeup?" Bess asked quickly.

"Oh, lots!" Lily said.

Bess smiled and hopped into a chair. "Then let's go for it," she said.

"But—" Nancy started to say.

Max clapped his hands. He pointed to the other two chairs. "Hurry, hurry. We have lots of work to do," he said.

Before Nancy knew it, they were sitting in makeup chairs with plastic capes around their shoulders.

"You have fabulous rosy red cheeks," Lily told Nancy.

Nancy was about to say "Thank you" when Lily slopped a handful of green goop on her face.

"Ugh!" Nancy gasped. From the corner of her eye she could see Max smearing silver goop on George's face.

"Yuck!" George cried.

Bess giggled. "I'm probably getting the pretty powder and the pink lipstick."

"Not in this scene, sweetie," Max joked. He reached out and rubbed Bess's face with purple goop.

"Eww!" Bess cried.

49

The girls stared in the mirror with their mouths wide open.

"And now for the hair," Lily said. She and Max held out cans.

"Oh, no," Nancy moaned. She squeezed her eyes shut. When she opened them, her hair was a weird shade of electric blue. George's hair was pink, and Bess's hair was bright orange.

"What do you think?" Lily asked.

George gulped. "We look like something out of a circus," she said.

"Fabulous!" Max said. He wiped his hands on a towel. "Now, how would you girls like to snack on a crunchy turtle?"

Nancy, Bess, and George looked at one another. Then they let out a piercing scream.

The door flew wide open. Mr. Bluestone and Vera rushed in. Behind them were Jason, David, and Mike.

"Is there a problem here?" Mr. Bluestone asked.

Mike pointed to Nancy and laughed. "You look soooo weird!" he said.

51

"Those aren't the kids for the clown scene," Vera told Lily and Max.

"They aren't?" Lily asked.

The clown scene, Nancy thought. So that explains it.

"These boys are," Vera said. She pointed to Jason, David, and Mike.

Mr. Bluestone tilted his head and looked at the girls. "Aren't you the girls from the pizza parlor scene?" he asked.

Nancy's blue hair bobbed as she nodded. "Yes, Mr. Bluestone," she said.

"Why did you come back?" Mr. Bluestone asked, confused.

Nancy decided to get right to the point. She hopped down from the chair and walked up to Mr. Bluestone.

"We wanted to find out if you and Vera ate up Harry," Nancy said.

"Harry the cameraman?" Max said.

"I think Harry's a turtle," Lily whispered.

"What are you talking about?" Vera asked Nancy.

"I heard Mr. Bluestone tell you to get rid of Harry," Nancy explained.

"And then we heard both of you say that you ate a turtle," George said.

Mr. Bluestone and Vera looked at each other. Then they began to laugh.

"You must mean this," Vera said. She reached for the box of caramels and shut it. Nancy read the words on the lid: Crunchy Munchy Turtles.

"They're called turtles because they're shaped like them," Mr. Bluestone explained.

"Vera would never hurt a real turtle," Max said. "She's got lots of pets."

"And Mr. Bluestone would never eat one either," Lily said. "He's a vegetarian."

"Some detective," Mike scoffed at Nancy. "You don't even know the difference between an animal and a piece of candy."

Nancy felt her face grow hot. She turned and walked quickly out of the trailer. Bess and George followed.

"Hey," Jason called out. "If you find Harry, let us know. There's a big turtle race tomorrow."

"Don't hold your breath," George called back.

As the girls walked back to their bikes, Nancy opened her blue notebook.

"The turtle thief is not Vera," she said. "Now I have no suspects at all."

"Nancy," Bess whispered. "I think we're famous already."

"Why?" Nancy asked.

"Because everyone's staring at us," Bess said.

"But why are they laughing, too?" George asked.

Nancy stopped walking. She covered her face with her notebook.

"Because we're still wearing our crazy makeup, that's why!" she cried.

"Oh, no!" Bess and George shouted.

7

Miss Snooty's Revenge

I wish I could disappear!" Nancy groaned.

The girls jumped on their bikes. People pointed and cars honked as they rode down Main Street.

"Look, Mommy," a little boy shouted. "The circus is here. Can I go?"

When Nancy reached her house, she ran straight inside. Her Labrador puppy, Chocolate Chip, jumped back and whined.

The Drews' housekeeper, Hannah Gruen, shrieked. "What happened to you?" she asked.

"It's a long story, Hannah," Nancy said. "A *real* long story."

Hannah helped Nancy scrub off the

makeup and hair goop. When it was completely out, Nancy sat down to dinner with her dad.

Carson Drew was a lawyer and often helped Nancy with her cases. He listened as Nancy told him everything about Harry.

"How many suspects do you have so far, Pudding Pie?" Mr. Drew asked.

"Zero, Daddy," Nancy said. "Now I'll have to look for more."

"Don't look for suspects," Mr. Drew said. He buttered his roll. "Instead, look for clues."

"But where?" Nancy asked.

Mr. Drew gave Nancy a wink. "Sometimes the clues come to you," he said.

"Well, they'd better come fast," Nancy said. "I have to solve this case by Monday—or else."

After dinner Nancy called Bess and George. She asked them to get permission to come to her house the next morning.

That night Nancy had trouble falling

asleep. She leaned over her bed and scratched Chip behind her ears.

I guess Lucy loves her pet just as much as I love mine, Nancy thought. I can't really blame her for being mad.

Nancy rolled on her back and stared at the ceiling. "But does she have to take it out on my whole school?" she mumbled.

Nancy woke up early on Sunday morning. She washed and pulled on a pair of jeans. She decided against the turtleneck sweater and chose a sweatshirt instead.

After a waffle breakfast, the doorbell rang. "I'll get it," Nancy told Hannah.

Nancy looked through the peephole. It was Bess and George.

"Hi," Nancy said, opening the door.

"Look what we found on your doorstep," Bess said. "The *Carlton News.*"

Nancy took the paper from Bess. "Why would I want the *Carlton News*?" she asked.

"Is Chip paper-trained?" George joked.

Nancy looked at the headline. "Star's Precious Pet Missing," she read.

The three friends sat on the doorstep. Nancy opened the paper and read the article out loud: " 'Thanks to Nancy Drew, Lucy Webb's turtle is gone.' "

"She always has to mention you, Nancy," George said angrily.

Nancy went on. " 'The turtle was last seen on Saturday afternoon,' " she read. " 'He has a hard shell with a star-shaped mark on it. There are two white dots on his head.' "

"She must have gotten a good look at Harry before he disappeared," George said.

"Brenda left the movie set early yesterday," Nancy said. "How could she know exactly what Harry looked like?"

"Unless," George said, "Brenda came back and stole Harry."

"Let's go to her house and question her," Nancy suggested.

"Go to Brenda's house?" Bess asked. "I'd rather go to a *haunted* house!"

"If we find Harry, it will be worth it," Nancy said. She looked at the newspaper and smiled. Her dad was right. Sometimes the clues really did come to you.

The girls rode their bikes to Brenda's house. Brenda was in her front yard, stacking copies of the *Carlton News*.

"Hello, Brenda," Nancy called as they walked into her yard.

Brenda pointed to the *Carlton News* in Nancy's hand. "I see you got my newspaper, Nancy. Did I spell your name right?"

"You always do," George snapped.

"How did you know so much about Harry, Brenda?" Nancy asked.

"Because I'm an awesome reporter," Brenda said with a grin.

Nancy sighed to herself. Brenda was a tough nut to crack. Then she had an idea.

"You left before Harry came out of his blue case," Nancy said quickly.

Brenda shook her head. "It's a pink case—" she started to say. Then she stopped herself.

Nancy smiled to herself. It worked! "How do you know Harry's case is pink, Brenda?" she asked.

Brenda stood up. She put her hands on her hips. "Are you saying that I stole Harry, Detective Drew?" she asked.

"I'm asking," Nancy said.

"Nicely," Bess added.

Brenda stuck her chin out. "Well, I don't have to answer. Who cares about your dumb detective cases anyway?" she asked.

"And who cares about your dumb newspaper?" George asked. She grabbed the *Carlton News* from Nancy. Then she walked toward the Carltons' trash cans.

"George—wait!" Nancy called as she ran after her.

"I'm putting this junk where it belongs," George said. She lifted the lid of the blue recycle can. Then she gasped.

"Nancy," George said. "Look!"

Nancy looked inside. She saw an empty bag of Turtle Chops just like the kind Rebecca had bought.

Nancy carried the bag over to Brenda.

"Give me that," Brenda said. She grabbed the bag from Nancy.

"You did steal Harry, didn't you?" Nancy asked.

"So what if I did?" Brenda asked. "It serves Lucy right."

"Why?" Nancy asked.

"Because she wouldn't let me interview her yesterday," Brenda said.

"Then why did you come back to the movie set later?" Nancy asked.

"I wanted to ask Lucy one more time," Brenda said. "But then I saw her giving you the pink case."

"We didn't see *you*," Bess said.

Brenda nodded. "I was standing behind a huge camera. I saw and heard everything."

"So you stole Harry just because Lucy wouldn't let you interview her?" Nancy asked.

"No," Brenda said, annoyed. "I did it because a story about a missing pet is much better than a boring interview."

Nancy couldn't believe her ears.

"You stole Harry so you could write about it?" she asked.

"I was going to give him back," Brenda admitted. "Harry is such a pest. Last night I found him swimming in my bubble bath."

The girls were silent as Brenda stacked the papers.

"I'll bet you make up all your silly stories," George finally said.

"Only when I have to," Brenda said. She flipped a paper open. "Like this one."

Nancy stared at the page. There was a picture of Lucy. Over it were the words, "Lucy Webb Thinks All Boys Are Icky!"

"It's not true," Brenda said. "But it makes a great story."

Nancy frowned. "It's dishonest, that's what it is," she said.

"And all boys aren't icky," Bess said. "Just Jason, David, and Mike."

Brenda shrugged. She picked up the papers and headed toward her house.

Nancy was glad she had solved the

case. There was just one thing she had to do.

"Brenda, wait," Nancy called. "Give Harry back to us. Right now."

Brenda looked over her shoulder. "I can't do that," she said.

"Why not?" Bess asked.

"Because," Brenda said with a grin, "I gave Harry away."

8
Show and Shell

Y ou what?" Nancy gulped.

"I gave him away," Brenda repeated.

"To whom?" Nancy asked.

"If you must know," Brenda said, "I gave him to Orson Wong."

"Orson?" Nancy asked.

"It was a swap," Brenda explained. "One turtle for one picture of Lucy. I needed it for my article."

The girls turned and walked quickly to their bikes.

"Good luck," Brenda shouted. But it was a mean good luck.

"Orson will never give Harry to us," Bess said as they hopped on their bikes.

"Maybe he gave Harry back to Lucy," Nancy said. "Let's go to his house and find out."

"I don't want to see any more little monsters," George said.

"Taco is probably back in his tank," Nancy said.

"I meant Lonny and Lenny!" George said.

When Nancy and her friends reached Orson's house, Lonny and Lenny were tossing a ball in the front yard.

"Where's Orson?" Nancy called.

The twins smiled.

"We know you *like* him!" Lenny said.

"This is important," George said. "Tell us where your brother is."

"And don't lie this time," Bess said.

"Okay, okay," Lenny said. "He's in the backyard. He's having an awk-ton."

"A what?" Nancy asked.

"You know," Lonny said. "Where a bunch of people try to buy the same thing."

Nancy turned to Bess and George. "I

think he means an auction," she said. "I went to one with my dad once."

"What's he selling?" George asked.

Lenny threw the ball in the air and caught it. "He's selling all his Lucy Webb stuff," he said.

"His souvenirs?" Nancy asked.

Lenny nodded. "Orson read in the *Carlton News* that Lucy thinks boys are icky. Now he's real mad."

"I had to help Orson carry all the stuff into the backyard," Lonny complained.

"And I had to get all the kids on the block to come over," Lenny grumbled.

"We're exhausted!" they cried together.

Nancy grabbed one twin by the shoulders. "Lonny—"

"I'm Lenny!" the boy said angrily.

"Okay, Lenny," Nancy said. "Is he also selling a turtle?"

"You bet," Lenny said. "We wanted to keep him, but Orson doesn't want anything that makes him think of Lucy."

Nancy felt her stomach flip. She had to stop Orson before it was too late.

"Let's go," she told Bess and George. They ran around the house to the back-yard.

Nancy counted seven kids in the yard. Orson stood on top of a picnic table. He held up an empty soda can.

"How much do I hear for this can of soda that Lucy drank from?" he called out.

Nancy could hear the kids mumbling to each other.

A girl raised her hand. "One bottle of my sister's nail polish!" she shouted.

Orson made a face. "Nah!" he said.

A boy with glasses raised his hand. "Two Winky Dinky bars!" he shouted.

"With nuts?" Orson asked, excited.

The boy nodded.

Orson smiled. "Sold! To the kid with the Winky Dinkys!" he cried.

Nancy watched as Orson exchanged the soda can for the candy bars.

"The next item . . . ," Orson shouted. He reached into his pocket. ". . . is Lucy's pet turtle."

Bess squeezed Nancy's arm.

Orson held up the turtle. "How much do I hear?" he asked.

Bess raised her hand. "A page of stickers. With glitter!" she shouted.

Orson rolled his eyes. "I don't think so," he said.

George's hand shot up. "A package of football cards," she shouted.

"Now you're talking," Orson said. He looked like he was about to yell "sold" when a boy shouted out.

"A package of football cards—and a brand-new football!"

Nancy, Bess, and George turned around. Jason, David, and Mike stood behind them.

"We want Harry for the turtle race," Jason said. "And we're going to get him."

"Oh, yeah?" Nancy asked. She raised her hand.

Orson pointed to Nancy. "What do I hear?" he asked.

"An autographed picture of Wammo the Magician," Nancy shouted.

"Wammo?" Orson asked.

Nancy nodded. Wammo was her dad's friend from high school. She could get the picture in just a few days.

Orson scratched his head. "I always wanted a picture of Wammo," he said.

Jason waved his hands. "I can get you a nickel that *Gonzo* the Magician pulled from his ear!" he yelled.

Excited murmurs filled the air.

Oh, great, Nancy thought. Gonzo is superfamous. He just had a big show on TV.

"Goodbye, Harry," George whispered.

But then Orson scowled. "Gonzo is a lazy dork," he shouted. "He stuffs everything up his sleeve!"

The kids in the yard gasped.

Orson pointed to Nancy. "Sold! To Nancy for a picture of Wammo," he said.

"Bummer," Jason grumbled.

The girls jumped up and down.

"You did it, Nancy," Bess said.

Nancy took the turtle from Orson. He had two white dots and a star-shaped mark.

"Lucy doesn't think boys are icky, Orson," Nancy said. "Brenda made the whole thing up."

"Then give me Harry back!" Orson demanded.

"Nope," Nancy said. "A deal's a deal."

Nancy carefully placed Harry in her pocket. Then she, Bess, and George rode their bikes straight to Main Street.

When they got there, Lucy was filming a scene outside the Big Scoop, an ice cream parlor on Main Street. After she finished, the girls walked over.

"What are you doing here?" Lucy asked.

"We brought you a present," Nancy said. She held up the turtle.

"If it's a new turtle, no thanks," Lucy sighed. "It'll never replace Harry."

"But it *is* Harry," George said.

"What?" Lucy asked.

"See?" Nancy said. "He has the star-shaped mark on his shell. And the dots—"

"Harry!" Lucy cried. She smiled at Nancy. "How can I ever thank you?"

"You can come to Carl Sandburg

Elementary School on Monday," Bess said.

"I was planning to come anyway," Lucy said. "I promised the principal. And a promise is a promise."

The girls gave one another high fives.

"There's just one small change," Lucy said.

"What?" Nancy asked, concerned.

A grin spread across Lucy's face. "This time I'm leaving Harry at home," she said.

Nancy laughed. From now on, everything was going to be Totally Perfect.

On Monday morning there was a special assembly for Lucy. She talked to the students about making movies.

After the assembly Lucy signed lots of autographs. Nancy wrote in her blue notebook.

The answer to "Where's Harry?" came just in time!
   I learned a lot about movies, turtles, and about Lucy, too. She

may be a big star, but she's just like any other girl who loves her pet.

I can't wait to see *Totally Tina*. I hope it has a real happy ending. Just like my mystery did!

Case closed.

Meet up with suspense and mystery in

THE CLUES BROTHERS

By Franklin W. Dixon

Look for a brand-new story every other month
at your local bookseller

 A MINSTREL® BOOK

Published by Pocket Books

1398-06

Do your younger brothers and sisters want to read books like yours?

Let them know there are books just for them!

THE NANCY DREW NOTEBOOKS ®

Look for a brand-new story every other month

Available from Minstrel® Books
Published by Pocket Books

1356-02